Goldilocks and the Wolf

Written by Hilary Robinson
Illustrated by Simona Sanfilippo

WAYLAND

Goldilocks ran from the Three Bears' house, down into Bluebell Wood.

She stopped to rest beside a stream and saw Little Red Riding Hood.

Goldilocks told her the story
of the bears she'd met that day.

Of how she'd tried their porridge...

...and why she'd run away.

Red Riding Hood said, "Are you feeling hungry? Would you like a bun?"

But as she laid the picnic cloth,
Goldilocks screamed, "Run!"

A wolf sat down between them
and said, "Buns! How kind of you!"

But the girls knew if they stayed there he'd try to eat THEM, too!

"Quick, run!" said Goldilocks again,
and both girls turned quite pale.

They went to hide behind a hedge,
but they spied the wolf's brown tail!

They ran and hid beside the pond.

Then Goldilocks gave a cry!

For peeping over the top of the reeds was the wild wolf's winking eye!

"I know," said Goldilocks.
"Let's take cover here."

But, over by the gate, they saw the wolf's brown pointed ear!

"Let's go!" they cried. "The riverbank has trees to hide beneath!"

But peeping through the rustling leaves they saw the wolf's sharp teeth!

Goldilocks said, "Follow me!
We'll race towards that farm.

"We'll try and find the Three Bears there
and raise the wolf alarm!"

"Listen," said Red Riding Hood,
"I've got a good idea.

"Let's go to my Grandmother's house.
She lives really very near."

But, as they ran, they heard a howl,
that echoed round the trees,
and when they turned around they saw
the wolf down on his knees.

"Don't go," he sobbed.
"Oh, please don't go.
Don't leave me all alone.

"No one wants to be my friend.
I'm always on my own!

"I'm just a friendly, gentle wolf.
I'm really very meek.

"And all I want to play with you
is a game of...

"...HIDE and SEEK!"

START READING is a series of highly enjoyable books for beginner readers. **The books have been carefully graded to match the Book Bands widely used in schools.** This enables readers to be sure they choose books that match their own reading ability.

Look out for the Band colour on the book in our Start Reading logo.

The Bands are:

Pink Band 1A & 1B

Red Band 2

Yellow Band 3

Blue Band 4

Green Band 5

Orange Band 6

Turquoise Band 7

Purple Band 8

Gold Band 9

START READING books can be read independently or shared with an adult. They promote the enjoyment of reading through satisfying stories supported by fun illustrations.

Hilary Robinson loves jumbling up stories and seeing how they turn out. Her life is a jumbled up lot of fun, too! Hilary writes books for children and produces radio programmes for BBC Radio 2 and, because she loves doing both, she really does feel as if she is living happily ever after!

Simona Sanfilippo loves to draw and paint all kinds of animals and people. She enjoyed reading illustrated fairytales as a child, and hopes you will enjoy reading these fairytale jumbles, too!